Yesterday, Today & Forever

Stories From the Heart

CALVIN BOWDEN

PUBLISHED BY FIDELI PUBLISHING, INC.

ISBN: 978-1-60414-969-2

For information, please contact

Fideli Publishing, Inc.:
info@fidelipublishing.com

www.FideliPublishing.com

Contents

Memories of My Boyhood on the Farm 1

Some Things are Forever 9

Visited by God 27

Uncle Willy's Garage Sale 69

Memories of My Boyhood
on the Farm

This is a true story about some of my experiences from the late nineteen twenties when I was five, living with my family on the Dave Redden farm in Nacogdoches County, Texas. I am now 92.

A five-year-old child does not remember all his experiences, but does recall those that were unpleasant or very pleasant, especially those that involved an adult who made him feel loved and accepted. I am anxious to tell you about such a person who came into my life in 1928, but first I will tell you about some of my other experiences that were not pleasant, but did help establish my sense of values and attitude toward life in general.

My dad was renting the Redden farm on three-fourth plan; he farmed it using his mules and implements, which allowed him to receive three-fourths of what he grew, particularly cotton, his money crop. While living on that farm, we had ample supply of food, because we always had a large garden, but our clothes were mostly old hand-me-downs, home made, or faded and patched store bought. If purchased new, they were the cheapest brand. We had very little money for items not required to grow crops, take care of the animals and poultry, or for buying items to eat we could not produce on the farm. The only thing I remember our dad buying that did not fall under these categories was a nickel's worth of chocolate mounds he brought home after a wagon trip to town. My dad never owned a car, never learned to drive one. Never could afford a farm tractor. But he loved to farm.

Times were hard for all sharecroppers. There were few jobs on surrounding farms after crops were laid by or harvested and sold. There were even fewer part-time jobs in town. Men welcomed work that paid enough for enough money to buy a sack of flour, or a bag of coffee or sugar. No work was too demeaning, never as bad as having to accept public assistance. If full-time jobs had been available, most farmers would have chosen to continue farming, because planting and growing was "in their blood". Living off the land was considered a noble endeavor, more rewarding than "living out of a paper sack" in town.

As a boy, I was never concerned about my family's finances and worn-out clothes, but did sense a longing for something I could not identify. I learned later the missing elements were called recognition and affection, both strong antidotes for rejection scourge, which handicapped me the rest of my life. During the education process, I learned that such a handicap is more prevalent in children from homes lacking in human warmth, as reflected by outward signs of affection such as touching, hugging, meeting of the eyes, loving words of encouragement and reassurance. It seems strange that a child who knows he is loved with the basic, instinctive love that all good mothers feel for their children could feel the need for more. Later in life, I felt guilty for feeling rejected and unloved, and prayed I would be forgiven for it. I wished I had expressed more words of love to my mother before she was taken away from us by age and illness. I feel I should have supported her more materially too, in spite of my knowing my parents had always seemed uncomfortable using words of love and affection.

When you are five years old, you lack the insight one needs to discuss such matters. That handicap, however, does not prevent any child from being overwhelmed when a gentle, loving adult like Miss Jewel comes into his life and makes him feel whole. Perhaps that is because everything is blown up out of proportion when you are a child. There are no unimportant things. When a loving, gentle person like Miss Jewel came into my life, it was as welcome as a lighted lamp in a window to a weary traveler during a dark, stormy night. But before I tell you more about Miss Jewel, I want to tell you about some of my experiences while living on the Redden farm that were not pleasant.

Our sharecropper house had no electricity, inside plumbing or bathrooms. Located near the fields where my dad grew cotton, peas and corn, it was where I spent my early years, the place where I had my first serious accident. I fell off a wagon loaded high with freshly picked cotton ready to be hauled to Buckner's cotton gin in town. Equipped with sideboards, it was about eight feet high. But it was parked in the cool shade of tall syca-mores, which made it a nice place for little boys to take a nap. The fall delivered a jolt hard enough to make me see stars. But the ground was soft sand, and no bones were broken, which would have been a disaster for a family with no money and no insurance. My next accident, however, delivered me to death's door.

As was the custom with poor farm families, I accom-panied my parents and siblings to the fields where they were working in the cotton crops, when the accident occurred. It was a busy time of the year when all hands were expected to do their share of the labor. In the shade where my mother and I had gone to get a drink of water, my mother placed my ragged straw hat on my head before returning to the field. Finding it not on straight, I jerked it hard around my head and a broken straw inside the old hat pierced my right temple artery.

The blood began spurting out with each beat of my heart, leaping some six to eight feet from where we were standing. The only time I had ever seen that much blood was at hog killing time. I believed I was going to die.

In spite of my life threatening injury, however, I was lucky again, or the beneficiary of divine intervention. I have often wondered which it was.

Only one person in the immediate area owned a car in 1928, and she lived a mile or more to her house through the fields, up a long lane, then across the Old Tyler Road through another field. The owner of the car, Mrs. Sandlin, I believe, was home. Another divine intervention? I have often asked myself that question.

I don't know how my parents moved me from the back field on the Redden farm to the home of the owner of that Ford Model T coupe, but they had only three options: carry me in their arms, haul me in the wagon, or ride me on one of our mules. But they did, and the kind lady transported this bloody sharecropper's son to Dr. George Barham's office in town where the artery was tied off. It has been tied off to this day, some eighty-eight years later.

It seems that tragedy and hard luck stalks the poor, because it was in that farmhouse where my younger sister, a crawling baby, had a near-death experience. She was crawling on the wood floor when she became choked, unable to breathe or swallow. Hearing her, our mother rushed over and picked her up to look into her mouth. Seeing nothing, she flipped her over to hold her by her feet and began shaking her. When nothing fell out, she placed the fingers of her free hand into her mouth and throat to search for the obstructions. Feeling something, she hooked her finger around it and jerked out. It was a large metal staple, the kind farmers used to build barbed wire fences. My sister was saved, and death was cheated again on the Redden farm, and our mother proved there are some things more important than nice clothes and inside plumbing.

After our experiences with a hot summer and death-defying accidents on the Redden farm, we were very pleased to have someone as positive and cheerful as Miss Jewell Coats in our home. My life, especially, was brightened like a dark, early monring is when the sun rises.

Miss Jewel came to live in our country home because it was the closest one to the one-room Union Cross School where she was going to teach the next school year. Her name quickly became identified with bright, positive living in our community, even more to our family. The memory of her tender touch, bright smile and recognition of my presence as an important human being has remained with me my entire life. Too young to go to school, I always waited for her return each day, eager to be boosted up again by her presence.

Miss Jewel did not choose to rent a room in our house because offered more conveniences than others in the area, but because it was only a short walk up the lane to the Old Tyler Road where the school was located. It was a shorter walk through the woods by Martin's pond where a friend and I were caught skinny-dipping one time by two bold girls from the community. The possibilities of what could have happened if we had dared to defy our moral teachings and waded out to the girls has been a matter that has always haunted me.

Many years later, after time and failing health took Miss Jewel from the world of the living, I was honored by a request from her daughter to write something that could be read at her memorial services. I did, and upon its reading I was lifted up and made happy as I was by her presence when she lived in our home on the Dave Redden farm many years before.

God bless you, Miss Jewel. Thanks for the memories.

Some Things are Forever

A man is confronted by the a mistake of his youth

Brenda Carlton was very concerned about her husband Reggie. He had always been a quiet man, but during the last couple of months he had become more withdrawn and moody, seldom hungry. Even more puzzling was the fact that he had not been with her during that time. He had always been an affectionate husband.

Her first concern was that he was seeing another woman, but the thought had made her smile. She could not imagine shy, gentle Reggie being so aggressive; unless there was a side of him she had never seen. The girls at the bridge club had told her all husbands are alike in that area of their lives. But Reggie had never been bold around her women friends.

She looked at him across the breakfast table as he slowly sipped his coffee with that familiar, far-off look in his eyes. He had hardly spoken to her since he got up from sleeping late.

"Reggie," she said. "'What are you going to do today? It would be a good time for us to do something together while the children at staying with mother and dad tonight."

He glanced at her and looked back at his coffee. "I'll do the same thing I usually do most Saturdays, I guess. Nothing." His eyes met hers. "I might -"He turned to look out the kitchen window.

"You might what?"

He shrugged. "Nothing."

"Reggie, is everything alright at the office?"

"Yes, why?"

"For some time now, you've acted like you're worried about something. Everything okay between you and your boss?"

"Things are so-so." He turned back to his coffee. "You know how old man Peyton is. He loves to make money, but doesn't like to spend it. He makes millions every year building roads and bridges, but won't give his comptroller-cashier a healthy raise. Sometimes I think I'd laugh if somebody came in with a gun and took all the cash he keeps in his special safe for cash purchases. He saves a bundle every time he buys equipment with cash."

"That's dangerous talk, Reggie. Be more assertive with Mr. Peyton. Ask him for a good raise."

"And get fired? A job with no raise is better than no job. "

"If you're not worried about something having to do with your job, you must be worried about our bills again."

He shrugged. "No use worrying about something that has to be."

"Then you've been thinking about going into business again. You've mentioned that many times lately."

"We don't have enough capital for that. There are lots of other things we can't afford too. A trip. New furniture."

He had said it with the same resignation he had said everything else the last couple of months.

"Tell you what." She managed a smile. "Why don't we pack a lunch and take a long drive in the county? We haven't done that in a long time."

Her suggestion caused no change in his somber expression. "Not today." He straightened in his chair as if steeling himself for a dreaded announcement. "Later, maybe. I was thinking about taking a drive out to see an old friend by myself."

His statement surprised her, because he almost never did anything outside the home without her and the children. She was now convinced he was deeply troubled. "Is this friend somebody I know? If it is, I'd like to go with you."

"No!" He said with surprising firmness. "It concerns something I have to work out by myself. After I hash it out, well … we'll see."

More concerned than ever, she began gathering up the dirty dishes and Reggie left the room in the direction of the bedrooms. Moments later she heard the shower running.

She shrugged, telling herself she would not pry further. A husband is entitled to his private moments now and then, doesn't he? She always went grocery shopping alone, didn't she?

Moments later, Reggie returned to the kitchen door dressed in khaki pants, sport shirt and golf cap. "I'm leaving. I'll be back in a couple of hours and we'll talk, okay?"

"Okay," she said nonchalantly, as if unconcerned about his mysterious trip. He walked to the garage out back and she resumed washing poets and pans and tried to stop worrying about her deepening concerns. But she could not forget the tense expression on Reggie's face, which until now had always been like an open book.

She watched as Reggie drove away in a westward direction, the way he had departed many times because the convenience store where they purchased gasoline was in that part of town.

She dried her hands, poured another cup of coffee and sat down, still haunted by the strange expression on Reggie's face and his disturbing statement about his wishing somebody would rob Mr. Peyton. The statement was completely out of character for Reggie, and the more she thought about it, the more concerned she became when she recalled the financial strain they had been in the last few years with the coming of their children, home repairs and a new car note. Inflation had more than offset the token raises Reggie had received.

Had she been pressing him too hard about asking for a raise? She had also been insisting on them needing new furniture and clothes. He never liked being pressured.

She reached for the phone on the wall. Martha and Joe Dixon had been their friends since high school. Martha could give her some good advice. Martha had always been a cheerful optimist, and never considered hurt feelings a reason to hold back good advice.

Her friend answered on the first ring and Brenda said: "Hi, Martha. Am I interrupting anything?"

"Yeah, honey. Joe's gone and I'm wrestling in the floor with the milkman. Hang up quick and call for a fire truck before we both explode."

"Knock it off, dreamer. I want to talk to you about a serious problem."

"What's the matter? Has Reggie gone cold on you?"

"That and a couple of other things. I'm really worried about Reggie. He's been in this quiet mood for weeks. Won't eat, won't talk to me about what's on his mind."

"Oh that. I can tell you what the problem is, dear."

"He talked it over with you and Joe?"

"He didn't have to, because I have to put up with that with Joe a couple of times a year. Married men get to thinking about being tied down to one woman, bills and kids while all those hot-to-trot pretty women are running around out there looking for a roll in the hay. Let Reggie dream on 'til he comes back to earth like I do my man. Just go on with what you usually do around the house and he'll get over it if he hasn't already let some pretty young thing get her hooks into him."

"Settle down, Martha. Reggie is more serious than Joe. Just keeps everything to himself."

"Wake up, kiddo. He's running around on you." She laughed. "It's the quiet ones you have to watch."

"A lot help you are."

"He's a man, isn't he?" She giggled.

"I'm afraid something is wrong at his job. He's very bitter about some things there. And all of a sudden this morning he drives off by himself. Wouldn't tell me where, or who he's going to see. What should I do?"

"Follow him, dummy. That's what I did one time when my Joe went mysterious with me."

"I can't do that. He's always been so good to the children and me. I read somewhere that a husband is entitled to a little quiet time away from his family now and then."

"That's what I'm talking about, silly. It's called the call of the wild. My guess is he's already found a she wolf that answered his call. Follow him and bust his bubble before it's too late."

"But—"

"But nothing. You've got your kids to think about. Face him and talk it out. And be sure to let me know when you have his funeral." She laughed and hung up.

Brenda returned to her coffee and found that just thinking about following her husband made her feel ill. "Martha and her gutter talk."

She ran her fingers over her hair and looked at her hands. They were not as soft as they used to be. Sliding them gently on her face and neck, she thought she felt places where her skin had begun to sag. She realized she was not as pretty as she used to be.

She went to the mirror in the bedroom and studied her reflection, grimacing upon seeing those places where she was sagging. She attempted placing her hands around her waist. She had grown older than she had realized. She must begin to exercise again, follow a strict beauty regimen.

Her thoughts were interrupted by the doorbell. *Who could be calling this early?* She opened the door and was shocked to find a worried looking Tom Peyton standing there. A small, bald man was with him. "Good morning, Mr. Peyton," she said as cheerfully as possible.

"Good morning, Mrs. Carlton," he replied gruffly. "I have to talk to Reggie. Is he home?"

Her heart began pounding. "No, sir. Won't you come in?"

"No, thank you." He nodded at the man with him. "This is Albert Wise. He's one of my auditors."

Brenda's legs suddenly became weak.

Mr. Peyton asked, "Can you tell me where I can find Reggie?" .

"I don't know were he went. Sorry. Is anything wrong?"

"Company business. It's very important that we talk to Reggie as soon as possible." He turned to go. "Tell him to call me immediately when be returns."

Brenda closed the door, very much wanting to call someone other than Martha. What had caused Mr. Peyton to be so upset on a day when the office was closed? Could Reggie's mood at the breakfast table have been caused by what Mr. Peyton was upset about?

She jumped when the telephone rang. She grabbed the receiver. "Yes?"

"Mrs. Carlton?" a man's voice said.

"Yes. Who is this?"

"Sheriff Gaines. Is Reggie home?"

"No, but—"

"When will he be back?"

"Don't know. What's this all about, sheriff? First Mr. Peyton comes by with his auditor looking for Reggie, and now you. I'm worried sick. What's going on?"

"You say old man Peyton came out? Well, I suppose he's not trying to keep it a secret."

"Keep what a secret?"

"They found a big shortage in an account that Reggie has access to. Nearly fifty thousand, Peyton said."

"Oh, my God! You don't think Reggie had anything to do with it, do you?"

"That's what we're trying to find out. Tell Reggie to call me. Gotta go now. Bye."

She sat down with the sheriff's words ringing in her ears. What to do? Determined not to sit, wait and worry, she picked up her purse and rushed out to her old Ford sedan in the garage, determined to find Reggie.

She saw something in the garage floor that made her pause. The loafers Reggie was wearing in the kitchen were in the spot where he kept his work boots. And the shovel was missing.

The first thought that came to mind was that Reggie had gone somewhere out in the country to bury the missing money. Oh, my God! Not my Reggie!

"I've got to talk to him now!"

But how? She did not even know where to start looking. She backed into the street, driving away in the direction Reggie took when he left. She would drive to the convenience store in case he had stopped to fill up. If he did, he might have said something to the clerk that would help her.

Risking a speeding ticket, she arrived at the store in half the time it usually took and rushed inside to talk to talk to the attendant, Mary Carpenter, a large, middle-age black woman. Mary was always friendly and helpful.

"Hi, Mary. Did Reggie stop here this morning?"

Mary gave change to a customer and closed the register. "And good morning to you too, Brenda. Slow down and catch your breath. Yes, he came by and filled up. What did he do, run off with the kids?" She smiled.

"I've got to find him. Did he say anything that indicated where he was going?"

"No, but he asked me if I knew where the Pisgah cemetery is."

"A cemetery? Oh my God! Which one?"

"I already said. Calm down. Pisgah cemetery is down a country road a ways from the community of Pisgah, about twenty miles north of here." She smiled. "I'm surprised you don't know where it's at, because it's the number one parking place for young white lovers."

"How do I find it?"

Mary took money from a customer for a pack of cigarettes and rang up the money. "Go out U.S. 59 'til you get to Pisgah at Farm Road Three Forty Three. Go left for about two miles 'til you come to a dirt road leading off to your right by an old, dilapidated barn. About a mile down that road you'll come to the cemetery. Watch close or you'll miss it. It's all grown up in weeds, bushes and trees. Nobody uses the old church or the cemetery any more. And since I'm too old to mess around any more, I don't know if it's used by lovers these days. Hope you don't find Reggie making out with one of your best friends." She smiled.

Brenda sped away, and when she turned into the farm-to-market road leading to the cemetery, she felt a strong sense of entering other peoples' worlds, and very guilty still for following Reggie. She drove slowly until she arrived at the old barn and turned into the country lane. When she saw the dilapidated church she pulled off the road into some tall weeds near a path of freshly pressed down growth of more grass and small bushes. Were they pressed down by Reggie's car? Her heart began beating faster.

She turned off the motor and looked at the solid wall of weeds and bushes ahead of her. She tried to see past the place where the other car's path disappeared, but the underbrush was too thick. She got out of her car and walked through the pressed-down growth toward the place where the other car's track disappeared under the big trees. By following the pressed down undergrowth, she would soon know if Reggie was the driver, and if he was, also find out what he was doing in such a remote, scary place. She thought she would die if she found him burying money.

She became even more tense when she saw a headstone through a small opening in the underbrush near where the other car had turned to go deeper into the taller timber and undergrowth.

Near collapse from fear, she wished she was not alone. If a strange man was driving the other car, she could be in danger of being robbed, murdered, or raped. There must be dozens of cars in the area like Reggie's.

She walked slowly and cautiously toward the other car, stopping every few seconds to listen for sounds. Arriving at the car, she looked it over carefully and concluded it was Reggie's Ford. She sighed with relief. But where was Reggie?

She jumped when she heard the sound of metal scraping against metal, or a stone. It had come from an area of undergrowth in front of Reggie's car, but she could not see Reggie.

Walking past Reggie's car she saw a small clearing. Walking toward it, she saw Reggie bending over the shovel. A twig snapped beneath her foot and he whirled, dropping the shovel.

"Brenda! What in the world are you doing out here?"

She raised her hand. "Now, don't be angry, Reggie! I knew you wouldn't want me interfering into your business, whatever it is. I didn't want to come, but I'm your wife and I love you. It's my duty to help you when you're in serious trouble."

"What made you think I'm in trouble?"

"Mr. Peyton and his auditor came by looking for you, and the sheriff called and said fifty thousand dollars is missing from company funds. Please tell me you didn't take that money."

She glanced at a spot of freshly disturbed red earth near him. "What did you bury there?"

"Which do you want me to explain first, that cleared grave site, or the missing funds from the office?"

She glanced at the rotting board with faded letters on it that was driven into the ground at one end of the freshly cleaned mound of dirt, and the area near it. "I came out here because of the scare about the missing money, but I'm now just as disturbed by that." She pointed.

"Okay, the money first. Yeah, ol' man Peyton is right for once. I did take the money."

"Oh, my God! What came over you, Reggie? You'll go to prison for sure!"

"Let me finish. I took it out of Peyton's special safe to buy some much needed heavy equipment at a bankruptcy sale that just opened yesterday. Peyton wasn't around and I didn't know where to find him. It was almost five o'clock, so it was buy or lose out situation. I could get it for half of what it would cost new. So I took the money from the safe that he keeps in his office for cash purchases, bought thee equipment and took the receipt home with me. The seller will deliver the equipment Monday morning and I'll give the receipt to Peyton."

"Then you didn't steal it!"

"Didn't you hear what I just said? Of course I didn't."

She sat down on a dead log with a long sigh. "Thank God!"

He sat down beside her. "I'm not a thief, but when I tell you about the grave, you'll probably think I'm a sentimental fool." He looked at the cleared mound. "I don't think a man can be sent to prison for that, but a wife's scorn can be almost as bad, if it's about another woman." He looked at her.

"It all depends. I'm listening."

"It's not the listening I'm concerned about. Try not to respond like a typical housewife, okay?"

He broke off the tip of a limb and tossed it away. "I met her long before I knew you, and our thing was over soon after."

"Your *thing*?"

"I didn't want to worry you with something that happened so long ago." He rose, motioning for her to join him. "No reason for you to know, really. Our brief friendship had nothing to do with you, or us."

"What was her name? Did I know her?"

"Agnes Hogan. She dropped out of school before you transferred in."

He stopped by the freshly cleared mound of earth. "About two months ago, I ran into a high school friend of mine that I hadn't seen in years at a job site, and in talking about the ones we knew in high school, he asked me if I'd heard what happened to Agnes Hogan that I dated a couple of times, mostly because I felt sorry for her. She had no friends. Her parents moved into our town from a farm near Pisgah. Her dad was a drunkard who beat her unmercifully every time she dated a boy and he found out about it. She wore old, hand-ne-down clothes. Never any makeup. She was nice looking, but shy and withdrawn. After I took her to a couple of ball games, she really began to hang on, and after a couple of beers in the city park one night, she got pretty wild. Afterward, she told me she loved me and wanted to marry me."

"And what did you say?"

"That I didn't love her, and wasn't ready to marry anybody. She cried like a baby, telling me nobody loved her, and that she'd never get married and have a family. Said she'd never get away from her mean daddy."

"Poor thing."

He nodded his head. "Yes. But what has made me feel so bad about her all these years, is knowing I took advantage of her that night when she was so vulnerable. I should not have done that, and I have prayed that God will forgive me for it."

She wanted to tell him she admired him for feeling the way he did for doing something most men would brag about, but thought it best to hear the rest of the story first. "

"After taking her home that night, I never went out with her again. A couple of months later, her parents moved her out of town and I never saw her again."

"But that wasn't the end of the story, right?" She pointed at the grave.

"My friend told me that when she told her parents she was pregnant, her father beat her and took her to a woman who performed an abortion. My friend said that when it appeared she was going to die from infection, she ran away from home and hitchhiked back to the Pisgah area to die." He shook his head. "I *really* felt guilty when he told me that. Ever since, I've kept remembering what she told me that night at the park about not being loved."

Her adrenalin surged. "The baby was yours?"

"It could've been, but my friend told me she never told anybody who the father was." His expression told her he was truly remorseful.

He said: "I wanted to do something that would let me stop feeling so guilty, and maybe let her know somebody did care for her as a friend. So I came out and cleaned off her grave after I found it a couple of weeks ago. And after I did, knelt by that crude headstone and prayed for forgiveness for abusing her and for all the other dumb things I've done. I was about to pull up a wild flower and push it in the fresh dirt to show her God loves her when I saw you. I should've talked to you first. You have every right to be mad at me. I love you and want to be married to you the rest of my life."

Mad at him? She was about to cry. She held his gaze a moment. "I'm a woman, so I'm jealous, but too impressed by what you've said and done, I'm not angry."

"Then you'll forgive me?"

"Tell you what. Meet me at the ice cream parlor in the mall on the way into town and buy me a big chocolate malt and I'll think about it. Like good ice cream, some things are forever."

She pulled up a tiny white flower and gave it to him. He pushed its roots into the loose, red soil near the headboard, backed up one step with bowed head, then picked up the shovel. Placing his hand on her arm, he walked by her side to her car.

Visited by God

Riding next to the window in the Gatlinburg, Tennessee, cable car on a sunny August day, I watched another car approaching the cable support tower from the opposite direction following its departure from the mountain top landing at the end of the line. The long, black transporter of tourists glistened brightly in the sunlight as it slowed down as it approached the incline leading to the support beam. All seats on it appeared to be filled.

Scanning the faces of those sitting on the side closest to me, I bolted upright when I spotted the familiar face of an elderly man with a sad, age-wrinkled face in the last seat. His wide, stooped shoulders told me he was a tall man. He was sitting alone on the seat. Although I had not seen him in many years, I had no problem recognizing Abe Stokes, my boyhood friend from the little town of Libbyville, Texas.

Suddenly seeing my close friend after fifty-two years who I thought was dead, was quite a shock, but after recovering from the unexpected sighting, I realized it was also comforting to see someone from my home town so far away with whom I had shared many experiences, pleasant and tragic. Our close relationship began in grammar school and continued through most of our senior year in high school. During that time, I shared his disappointments, temporary highs and his ultimate tragedy. Encountering him as I took my first trip away from my Nashville retirement home alone since my beloved wife Becky died made the occasion even more moving. I moved my face closer to the window as the other car moved slowly over the peak of the cable support no more than twenty feet away. I waved my arms and called out, "Abe! It's me, Bill Hadley, your friend from Texas!" He did no hear or see me.

I struck my knuckles against the window, ignoring the surprised looks from the other passengers.

My tall, stoop shouldered friend with the weary face and white hair did not see or hear me, and moments later his car became very small as it continued on its way to the Gatlinburg station.

I rushed forward and asked the car's operator, "How long does this car stay on the mountain?"

"About an hour, or until all passengers return to the car ready to leave," the woman replied.

"Can you talk to the operator of the one we just met? There's somebody on it I have to see."

She picked up a mike. "Which one?"

"The elderly tall man with white hair sitting in the last seat on this side. Tell the operator to ask him to please wait at the landing 'til this car gets back, because his old friend Bill Hadley from Libbyville wants to talk to him."

She pressed a button and repeated his message. "Anything else?"

I shook my head and returned to my seat to think about the man I would talk to upon my return to Gatlinburg. What an exciting reunion that would be.

During the early years of Abe's life and afterwards, I had befriended him many times in an attempt to lift him up from his despondent state, but had not talked with him since he was sent out of Libbyville many years ago. He had considered me to be his special friend from elementary school days, beginning in nineteen forty eight. I was the only one in our class who was kind to him, in spite of his poverty-stricken circumstances and his reluctance to make friends. Coming to school barefooted wearing ragged overalls and faded, torn shirts, he was shunned and laughed at by his fellow classmates. He would never have participated in the games we played during recess had I not insisted. In spite of his reluctant participation, however, he remained very bashful and withdrawn, seeing himself as an unworthy outcast among other children who wore nice clothes and delivered to school by their mothers driving new Fords and Chevrolets.

As a result of my telling my parents about Abe, they felt sorry for him and purchased him one pair of new shoes, a couple of shirts and one pair of overalls which they allowed me to deliver to him in his home. For doing that, I was called "Preacher" by our fellow students. In spite of his limited supply of new clothes, Abe was still considered by most students to be backward and dumb.

Because of my closeness to Abe, I remained well informed of the happenings in his day-by-day activities from his first days at school to the time of his greatest disaster. What he did not tell me, my friends and family did. Our family grocery store was a very effective place for gathering and disseminating information. In addition to this source, I was asked by the Libbyville Press editor, following Abe's great disaster, to delve deeper into his life's experiences for information that would be published in a report about Abe's life which he would share with our high school alumni newsletter.

Abe's sudden appearance told me he still carried the burdens heaped upon him by family circumstances, the worst of which was low self esteem. I recalled, however, how he had done better than most expected in interpersonal relationships after I persuaded him to start playing basketball after school. Not long after that, I persuaded the coach to place him on our team.

I had often thought of Abe through the years, and wondered what had become of him. After his parents died and his brothers and sisters moved from Libbyville, my relatives there had heard nothing more about him. Now, suddenly, he was back in my life, and if he got my message and waited for my return, I would learn all about his life since we last saw each other in that hospital room. Until then, I had only memories to prepare me for our reunion.

Abe Stoke was raised in a dilapidated clapboard house near a large sawmill on the outskirts of Libbyville which was located in the tall pine country of East Texas. Although his full name was Abraham, everybody called him Abe. Some said it was because he looked like Abe Lincoln. Others believed he was named after the Great Emancipator with the hope his entire family, like the slaves, would somehow be freed from grinding poverty and endless struggle.

It seemed Abe was born tall and kept growing. The girls in school had always made fun of him in grammar school and beyond, because he was so stooped and awkward looking. And bashful. Some said he was shy because he was dumb, but others believed it was because he had always seen himself as being so much unlike his classmates in his faded, worn out cloths. Others believed it was because he was ashamed of his father, the town drunk who seldom worked. Abe had been burdened with family shortcomings since birth.

As a freshman in high school, Abe was taller than the other boys at six feet two, and if he had not been stoop-shouldered, he would have been at least two inches taller. Students who teased him believed he was stooped because he wanted to be more like his classmates, and not be the butt of so many jokes and pranks. I believed the main cause of his personality problems, however, were his continued abuse at the hands of his father, and lack of affection from his illiterate mother.

During Abe's elementary school years he took menial jobs to help support his poverty stricken family, and when not working, he helped his mother with the house chores and tended the family garden. If he was paid anything for doing odd jobs, it was taken from him by his father who bought more whiskey with it. Their limited funds for the purchase groceries they could not grow came from the earnings the mother for sewing and washing for others and hidden where her husband could not find it. The town's largest employer, the Libbyville sawmill, refused to rehire the father following an accident he caused following a night of heavy drinking that killed a fellow worker.

Abe had seven brothers and sisters, all younger than him; and since much of earnings of Abe and his mother were spent on whiskey by the father, there wee times during the fall and winter months when there was not enough food for all. Abe, however, never showed any signs of bitterness toward either parent. If his mother appreciated Abe's lack of complaints and his small contributions, she never indicated it.

The family's light came from kerosene lamps. The mother cooked on a wood burning stove, and heat was provided by a fireplace, both fueled by free wood from the sawmill's scrap pile.

In spite of his family's circumstances, Abe came to school fairly regularly; and much to everyone's surprise, made passing grades in all subjects. When I told him how much I admired him for that, he looked at me and told me shyly that he did it so I and Mrs. Davis, his English teacher, would not be disappointed in him. He said we were the only people at school who treated him like he was somebody, and the only ones who had visited him in his home.

By the time our freshman year arrived, I noted additional signs of discouragement in Abe's demeanor. I had continued to befriend him in spite of my being told by other students I was wasting my time. In talking to him, I sensed that I was not allowed to share Abe's innermost thoughts and concerns as I had before. It was as if he was afraid to allow anyone to see through the protective shell he had thrown up around himself to avoid continued ridicule. I feared he might drop out of school and fall into the depressing, hopeless lifestyle of his parents, but he did not. Since he had never had a girl friend, or talked to me about girls, I thought that might be his new source of concern.

When some of my friends asked me why I continued to take such a personal interest in Abe's welfare. I told them it was because of some things I had heard our preacher say in his sermons, and scripture read to us in Sunday school. After that, more of my friends called me Preacher. They told me I was too sentimental, that my time would be better spent on more deserving classmates. I disregarded their advice, and continued to encourage Abe to participate in high school sports, beginning with after school games. After much private coaching from me in all sports offered at out school, it was apparent he was most suited for basketball.

Abe's eye-muscle coordination was outstanding, and his stamina had no equal, so with time, his height and long reach made him the star of our team, earning him the first widespread recognition in public affairs. He played first string all through his sophomore year, but outside the gym his life continued to be colorless and depressing.

I expected his new popularity on the basketball court would cause him to overcome his shyness and become popular with the girls, but it did not. The negatives from his childhood were too strong.

Abe continued playing basketball well, however, in spite of not fitting in well with his fellow players and pretty girls. Eventually, however, a large, freckled face girl began flirting with Abe, and if he had encouraged her, she most likely would have been as free with her favors with him as she was with other boys. Abe continued to ignore her, but began looking longingly at the beautiful Marie Tidwell each time she appeared at a game, or passed him in the hall. With clear, fair skin, shapely figure, sparkling brown eyes and long black hair, she was the most attractive girl in our class, and she had a sparkling personality to match her beauty. Daughter of a local banker, she associated only with sons and daughters of the small, closely knit families of the business and professional class of Libbyville. Sons of laborers and mill workers were never seen with her, or at social events she attended. When she walked by Abe and I in the hall one day after he lettered in basketball, I nudged him and asked why he didn't ask her to have a Coke with him sometime, he gave me a shocked look and walked hurriedly away. It was clear that he considered her to be so far above his social class that he could never consider himself worthy of such an honor.

Because Abe had been the high scorer on our conference winning team that year, the event called for Marie to give him a ribbon with a kiss and dance with him. Wearing one of my coats and a white shirt and tie, he stooped down to accept a peck on his cheek with a frightened expression and a nervous smile. Abe could not dance, but reluctantly accepted the challenge after much urging by his fellow players, and stumbled part way around the narrow space without doing serious harm to Marie's little feet before she abruptly jerked her hand out of his and hurried back to her chair.

Abe remained in the dance area, stooped with arm out as he was before he was so rudely abandoned. It became very quiet in the room before his team mates began applauding and the band began playing "For He's a Jolly Good Fellow." With bowed head, Abe dropped his arm and returned to his chair among his teammates.

In spite of his embarrassing experience at the hands of Marie, Abe's fascination with her did not falter. To the contrary, it appeared that his holding her in his arms for such a brief time had deepened the affection he felt for her. That was made clear by the way he looked at her at school and during basketball games. When Marie laughed and beamed with the fortunate boys who were always around her, Abe quickly looked away with a pained expression. He told me during the beginning of our senior year that he knew she would soon be taken as a wife by one of her rich boy friends. He said it sadly, but not resentfully, telling me he was convinced her marriage to anyone not wealthy and popular would be robbing her of all the nice things she deserved.

When Abe finally gathered up enough courage to speak to Marie on the sidewalk downtown, he removed his cap and said, "Morning, beautiful lady." All he got for his unaccustomed boldness was a toss of her head and a view of her pretty backside when she walked past him. Between classes the next day, she told my girlfriend, Becky Sutton, about the encounter and said she hoped none of her friends had witnessed the incident.

To everyone's surprise, Abe attempted to talk to Marie again the next time he met her downtown, and in spite of another rebuff, he continued to tip his cap and speak to her each time he met her on campus or downtown. He did not attempt another conversation; however, apparently convinced his humble station in life did not entitle him to the privilege. In spite of her continued rejection, his affection for her was not diminished. Nor was it affected by the rumors about her virtue that began circulating like a wild grass fire around the campus. He told me he could not believe any girl so beautiful could have a moral weakness. One day, when angered by statements overheard about her morality made by a fellow student, only the intervention by the passing principle prevented Abe from striking the student. When I asked my girlfriend about the prankster's statement, she smiled mischievously and shrugged. I took that as a confirmation of the validity of the rumors, but I did not tell that to Abe.

Near midterm of our senior year, the local constable found Abe's father dead under a bridge and Abe promptly dropped out of school and got a job driving a lumber truck for Libbyville Lumber Company. The principal, I and our basketball coach pleaded with him to come back to school, but he sadly shook his head and climbed back into his truck. I also went by to plead with his mother, but all she said was how blessed she was to have a man in the family that would work full time to support her and the other children. I advised the principal of her response and he took a last look at Abe's report card filled with A's and B-pluses, and filed it away.

When his dad died, Abe inherited his grandfather's old fiddle, which he had been forbidden to touch up to that time. I never knew why, because his father could not play it and apparently had no desire to learn. The instrument needed new strings, but for some time Abe did not have the cash to buy them. When he mentioned the problem to me, I drove my dad's car to the first town that had a music supply store and purchased strings, a new bow, tuning horn and resin. After that, neighbors and passersby at night reported hearing the squeaking strings of the old fiddle long after everybody living close by had gone to bed. No one understood his fascination with the old fiddle, but concluded that in it he had found something he loved that did not reject him, thereby causing him to feel worthy at last. So now, something else was added to his short list of things he loved: Marie Tidwell, basketball and the fiddle.

Abe told me that when his mother complained about all the squeaking sounds when he attempted to play, he placed the instrument in its old case and walked down the road to a secret place in the woods to practice. He continued going there after work and on weekends until he could play well. He told me he loved it so much, he sometimes returned to his secret place late at night to play by candlelight. Out of sight and beyond hearing range during that time, his neighbors forgot about Abe and his old fiddle.

On the job, Abe continued to be withdrawn, seldom talking to anyone other than co-workers and customers. After he was transferred to wholesale deliveries, he was seldom seen during the week in Libbyville.

Months later, however, when it came time for our annual Patriots' Day fiddle contest on the first Saturday in July, Abe arrived at the judges' table next to the raised platform to tell them he was a contestant. Participants and spectators near the judges' table turned disbelieving eyes on the tall, black clad young man with the old black fiddle case under his arm. When others in the audience realized what was about to happen, a hush fell over he crowd, and for a moment I feared Abe might revert to his former shy self and leave.

Mayor Sam Willet and the chief judge hesitated, apparently undecided about whether to allow Abe to play. Something about Abe's serious demeanor must have caused them to shrug and add his name to the list of contestants.

Abe looked longingly at the boys and their dates in the crowd milling about beyond the chairs, laughing and talking excitedly. The older spectators sitting in metal chairs just beyond Becky and I, were quietly watching the contestants near the platform, anxious for the music to begin.

One of Abe's former classmates, Thad Wilson, yelled, "Hey, Abe! Where's your girl?" Thad's friends laughed.

Abe pretended he didn't hear the question, but upon noting Thad's date was Marie Tidwell, he smiled shyly and approached him. "Hello, Thad. How's the team doing?" His eyes remained on Marie.

Thad took a swallow of his coke. "Not so good lately, Abe. I don't know what's wrong."

Son of the local pharmacist, Thad had always been popular with the girls and of late had been going steady with Marie. Abe had told me he had seen them together many times and had heard talk about them driving into the country at night. Abe knew about Thad's reputation with girls, and had recently told me he was worried about Marie.

"Hello, Marie," Abe said finally.

Marie's expression reflected her surprise at Abe's boldness. "How's your job going, Abe?" she asked with a cautious glance around. "Have you talked lately to any interesting girl wood sawyers in that lumber you're hauling?"

Thad and his friends burst out laughing and Abe's face flushed. He stopped smiling.

"Cheer up, Abe," Thad chided. "That tall, freckle faced girl in our class that's built like a lumberjack is here and she's looking for a man."

Abe continued to give Marie a sober look. She turned to give him a teasing look. "Abe, can you really play that old fiddle?"

Abe's face lit up. "Wait here and you'll soon find out. I'll dedicate my first number to you."

Thad asked, "What will your first number be, 'Stranger in the Real World'?" More laughter from his friends. He tugged on Marie's arm. "Come on, honey. Let's get away from this creep and take a ride to where we can have some real fun."

Abe's smile faded as Thad and Marie disappeared into the crowd. He looked down at the fiddle case and sighed like a man freshly reminded of his inadequacies. He sat down beside the other fiddlers to await his turn to play.

The fiddlers preceding Abe were older men. They played the standard fiddle tunes from the past, accompanied by two rhythm guitars and a bass fiddle. The audience applauded enthusiastically after each number.

I was told later by one of those who had been sitting up front that Thad and his friends had stopped in the shadows to wait for Abe mostly out of pity. They really did not believe he could play well enough to be part of the festivities. Abe's family must have thought that tool, because none of them were present.

Abe's turn came and the audience fell silent as he slowly climbed the steps of the performers' platform. Turning, he looked out at the large crowd as if he might be having second thoughts about playing, and then removed his old fiddle from its beat up black case. He told the backup players, "For my first number, I'm gonna play You Are My Sunshine in D, and I'm dedicating it to the pretty lady named Marie that jus left."

A murmur ran through the crowd and a girl giggled. Those who were seated looked around the lighted area hoping to see Marie. I hoped she had not gone so far already that she did not hear Abe's dedication over the loudspeakers hanging in the trees.

Skeptical expressions turned to shocked amazement as Abe began to play, softly and smoothly, double noting at the appropriate places. There were no missed notes, no squeaking of strings as a result of a misplaced bow or finger, no loss of rhythm. On the second course, an old man in the first row began singing the words to the song and was joined by another, then another, until most of those present wee singing the familiar song.

Abe's expression remained one of sincere concentration, smiling when the spectators began singing. It appeared his playing had transported him into a kinder world where he had found acceptance and beauty.

When Abe finished playing, the spectators stood and applauded wildly, making it impossible for Becky and I to move forward and congratulate him. Someone called out, "Great, Abe! Play us another one!"

Abe blushed and bowed, waving his bow at the happy spectator. When the applause stopped, he told the guitar players, "Key of G" and began "Westphalia Waltz". The backup players fell in behind him and the sweet sounds of the familiar piece filled the lighted area and beyond, leaving no spectator untouched by its beauty.

With enthusiastic applause still filling the park at the end of the number, Abe began a fast Irish reel without announcing the key. He therefore played alone on the first few bars, but those accompanying him quickly found their places and joined him as some spectators moved into the isles to begin dancing, clapping their hands or patting their feet. A rebel yell was heard. Abe played as only the most inspired and gifted could, and his face glowed with pride and happiness like I feared I might never see thee. Abe had, at last, found acceptance as a valuable human being for which he had always yearned.

A movement near the end of the back row of seated spectators caught my eye, and I saw Marie Tidwell quietly studying Abe. She turned suddenly and walked back into deeper shadows.

The audience demanded an encore, and after playing "Boil Them Cabbage Down", the judges insisted on getting on with the remainder of the program. Perspiring profusely, Abe climbed down and returned his fiddle to its case. Pushing through a throng of admirers, I shook his hand and told him how much I admired him, and Becky embraced him and kissed his cheek. From that date, Abe was called The Fiddling Man, and when he played anywhere after that, he performed with the same enthusiasm he had displayed at the contest which had earned him a blue ribbon and a free lunch at the City Cafe. The most important gift, however, was self confidence, and the belief that life had real meaning after all. He spoke to those he met and talked to those he knew, always smiling. In view of his mass transformation, it seemed impossible that the tragic events which followed could have been possible. I often wondered how anybody with the ability to make others happy with their music, could be influenced by anyone or any power to do something so unlike the person Abe had become.

Abe continued to work at the lumber company and at night play contemporary country and western music at dances and special occasions of all kinds. He and the backup band also began broadcasting bluegrass music over the radio station at our county seat. During that time, he was seen in public with two different girls, one of them being the tall, buxom, freckled one that had pursued him for some time. The other girl, smaller and not as bold, was more attractive, but not as pretty as Marie. After a couple of dates with each, however, Abe stopped seeing them. He told me later, that if he could not have the girl he wanted, he would go out with none of them. I knew he meant Marie Tidwell.

Marie continued to avoid Abe on the streets of Libbyfille, but he continued to see her at dances where he and his band provided the music. On those occasions, however, she appeared not to notice his greetings. His face saddened each time she appeared with a different boy, always cheerful and smiling. She and Thad had broken up soon after the fiddling contest, and she had begun dating other local boys.

In spite of Marie's aloofness, Abe continued to smile and speak each time they met at public gatherings. After each meeting, his choice of a song to play was a sad one, usually about a lost love or a lover's betrayal.

After once of those occasions, I told him he should walk over to her and tell her how pretty she was, and how he felt in her presence. "Ask her for a date,"

He had sighed and said, "I don't have a car."

When I saw Abe in passing several days later, I learned he had not followed through on suggestions. He was still keeping his pent-up emotions of love and affection locked inside himself as before. A couple of months later when we met on the street, he told me he would have to be satisfied with playing the fiddle and seeing Marie in public gatherings in hopes she would eventually return his greetings and talk to him. When I told him again how he must be more positive and believe in himself more, his eyes met mine and he said, "You really think she might stop and talk to me if I got pushy?"

I nodded. "Courting a girl is like learning to play a fiddle. One has to be persistent. Play the same tune over and over. Even if the fiddle has been played before." I realized, too late, that I had said too much.

"Playing a fiddle don't hurt it none."

I placed my hand on his shoulder. "Of course not. But not believing in yourself hurts you. Move in. Be more aggressive."

I did not want to do or say anything that might destroy his idealistic view of the girl he loved. If he were fortunate enough to win her affections, I hoped he did not discover things about her that would jerk away the pedestal she was standing on in his view. I shuddered when I thought of what he might do if that happened.

Abe was asked to join anther country and western dance band and tour the country, but he declined. Everyone but me wondered why. I knew it was because he did not want to go where he could not see the girl who might some day allow him to court her.

When Abe turned nineteen, he left his mother's home and rented a room at Mrs. Flower's rooming house. He began to dress up more and go to the Methodist church, to which my family and Marie's family belonged. Marie had remained in Libbyville following graduation and had continued to be very popular with the boys, which caused more gossip about her virtue. If Abe placed any value in such talk he did not show it. He saved his money and purchased a used Dodge sedan which he pampered as much as he did his fiddle. Soon after that, he joined the Methodist church, and on he third Sunday following that occasion, he did what he had wanted to do for a long time, and I was close enough to hear what was said.

He approached Marie as she walked alone to her parents' car after church. Pulling at the collar of his white shirt made tighter by a blue tie, he smiled and said to her, "Hi, Marie. Got a minute to spare?"

She stopped and looked up at the face towering Abe, whose expression told me he was shocked to see what Becky and I had already noticed from seeing her in the sanctuary. Her face was pale and drawn and there was a look of sadness in her eyes.

"Hi, Abe," she said with a faint smile. "You look nice."

Abe's face lit up. "Thank you. And you're as beautiful as ever." He looked at her pale cheeks. "I hope you're well."

"I'm okay. Thanks for caring." She glanced nervously at the people passing by.

"Nice day, ain't it?" he said. "Ah, *isn't* it?"

"Yes it is."

"Could I drive you home?"

Great! He had finally popped the question.

"Thank you, but I'm with my parents. Bye."

She walked to the family car as the flabbergasted Abe watched with a frozen smile. He remained still, apparently oblivious to the passing church goers. He glanced around finally, as if to see if anyone he knew had witnessed his achievement.

He found the preacher watching him, and when Abe began walking away, Reverend Caruthers overtook him. "Good morning, Abe." He had a kind voice.

Abe smiled. "Mornin', sir."

"I've noted your attendance every Sunday since joining our church, and I've been anxious to tell how much I admire you for that. I hope it's because you've found comfort in my messages in the house of a loving and forgiving God."

"Yes, sir, I have. It gives me comfort to know I can sit in there with all those nice folks and be greeted like I'm somebody."

"That's one of the rewards for sharing the company of other Christians, young man. I feel your family would also be made to fill more fulfilled if they would also attend. Think you can bring them with you next Sunday?"

"My parents never went to church, and since my dad died, I know my mom won't get religious. She and my sisters don't have nice enough clothes to wear if she did."

"Our church has a program that helps people of the community who are in need. It has been taking groceries to your mother and siblings. I'll ask them to take them some clothes appropriate for Sunday wear."

"I've helped them as much as I can since I moved out. But when mom told me about them getting food stamps, a welfare check for my two youngest sisters, and medical help through Medicaid, I'm thinking she may be better off than I am. If I can buy church clothes, I believe she can too. But I do appreciate the church helping them."

"I'll tell our public assistance that, and about her other resources. Our supplies are limited. About the clothes problem. Coming to church isn't about clothes. It's about souls. What's in a person's heart is what counts."

"I thought that too, Mr. Preacher, but in the past, I've known lots of church going folks who didn't seem to have got the message yet."

"I heard talk of your troubles growing up and at school, and I've prayed that some day you'd find acceptance and joy. That's why I'm so happy you accepted the

Lord as your personal savior. God bless you." He offered his hand.

"Thank you for your kindness, preacher," Abe said with a glance at Marie in the back seat of her parent's car as it drove by.

Reverend Caruthers' eyes twinkled. "She's a beautiful young lady."

Abe nodded. "A man needs somebody that makes him complete, pulls him up. He needs a good wife to love."

"I agree. Come to my study sometimes and we'll talk more. Good day."

Abe told me later it was the first time he had opened up to someone besides me, and that he loved the preacher for caring enough about him to speak to him in public.

Abe had just reached his car when Thad and several other boys from the sanctuary approached him.

"Hey, Abe," Thad said. "Rusty and I want to give you a little friendly advice. Stay away from that tramp Marie Tidwell. She's looking for a sucker."

Abe frowned. "A sucker?"

"You don't know anything about women, do you?" Thad said. "Always looking at her like a sick puppy, hoping she'll start smiling at you like she does all the rich boys in town. Didn't it strike you as being odd that she started being friendly with you all of a sudden? Regardless of what you think of us, we're your friends. That's why we want to warn you."

"You didn't act like you wee my friends in school."

"That was before you became our star basketball player and began acting more like a regular person. And now you're our town's star attraction with that fiddle."

"What's with you? I remember when you and Marie were the talk of the school campus, and town."

"That's before I smartened up, fiddle boy. I can't be seen any more with that slut. She's also a pot head and a drunk. And she's pregnant. That's why she's looking for some guy to marry her. That way, it'll make her look respectable again. None of her lovers will marry her because they don't want to support another guy's kid. She doesn't even know herself who the father is."

Abe struck Thad in the face with his big right fist, knocking him down. Rusty attempted holding Abe's arms, but Abe shoved him aside and turned back toward Thad as he climbed to his feet.

Thad said, "That didn't change anything, you big ape. She's still a slut."

Rusty said. "Stop it, guys. Not in front of the church!"

I rushed over and grabbed Ape's arm, telling him, "Don't let Thad's big mouth get you put in jail. He got your message."

Abe's eyes met mine. "Do you believe what he said?"

"I'm not God. I don't judge."

A car stopped at the curb and Abe was surprised to find Marie looking at him from the back seat of her parents' car again. I had seen her dad turn around at the end of the block, and suspected he had done it at Marie's request. Her eyes swept over the other boys and the disheveled Thad. When she looked at Abe, her eyes told me she knew what had happened and why. Then she was gone, and Abe walked to his car.

Others who witnessed the incident told me later that they doubted Abe had fully comprehended the full meaning of Thad's remarks, but Abe's expression had made it clear that the confrontation had placed still another burden on his shoulders that was beyond his control. He told me later that after the fight, he had stopped playing happy music at dances, concentrating instead on the slow, sad ballads about lost loves and a poor man's burdens. Others told me he had become more like his former self, seldom speaking or smiling.

Abe continued working for the lumber company, and on two occasions was observed quietly watching Marie as she attended to errands downtown. She always returned his gaze and smiled, but her eyes were sad. Some two weeks later, she was observed parked outside a dress store located near the lumber yard, and when Abe walked from the lumberyard toward the City Cafe across the street, she met him on the sidewalk.

Abe stopped, but for several moments did not speak. Then, "Mornin', Marie."

"Good morning. I've been wanting to thank you for what you did for my sake that Sunday at church."

"Oh, that," he said. "Thad owed me a little gambling debt. I —"

She placed her hand on his arm. "Thanks, Abe, for wanting to spare me. But I'm afraid I don't deserve it after the way I treated you in the past. I now know how it makes a person feel when he's talked about."

He glanced at the café. "Care for a cup of coffee?"

"Now? Here?"

He appeared crestfallen. "If you'd rather not, I'll understand."

"I only meant that I didn't know whether you'd want to be seen with me after what those boys told you. I know what they've been saying around town."

His expression brightened. "As far as I'm concerned, those guys were just spreadin' fertilizer. Fertilizer never spoiled the beauty of any flower. Let's get some coffee."

For the next week Abe and Marie were seen together every day at various places, including church on Sunday. Abe told me he could feel the eyes on them as they walked down the isle to the front pew, and heard the whispered remarks of those seated nearest them, but it did not disturb him because he was a contented man. That was reflected by an expression of genuine happiness on his face. However, it was more difficult to interpret the expression on Marie's face, but if Abe saw a hint of forced acceptance there, he apparently chose to ignore it.

I found out later, that on Tuesday of the second week of their courtship, Abe took Marie to his special place on the edge of town, where their chair was the trunk of a giant, dead oak tree near several blooming dogwoods and a climbing wisteria vine. Marie told her mother that Abe took his fiddle and played "Beautiful Dreamer".

Abe and Marie returned to his secret place several times after that, and each time he did not return to the rooming house until very late each night. On one morning following one of those nocturnal visits, Abe and Marie were observed entering Reverend Caruthers's residence, and by noon the word was all over town about the wedding that was about to get underway in the church. Shortly thereafter, two carloads of boys wee seen driving slowly by the lumberyard. After several drive-bys, they stopped and got out to wait in silence by the lumberyard's entrance.

When Abe drove up in a truck at five, the boys signaled him to stop. Abe stopped and watched in dreaded silence as they approached.

"Hi, Abe," Thad said cautiously.

Abe nodded. "What are you and your fellow gossipers up to this time?"

"Now, don't lose your temper again, Abe," Thad said. "In spite of what happened at the church, we're all still friends of yours. We all played basket ball together, remember?"

"Out with it. I've got work to do."

"We still don't want to see you make the biggest mistake of your life, Abe. You're a nice guy. I know we've treated you bad in the past and said some pretty dumb things about you. But damnit, Abe, you don't understand what you're getting into, marrying Marie Tidwell. Believe me, she'll never change. Some women are like that with guys and can't help it. And as I said before, she's looking for a man willing to marry her in her condition."

For a moment, Abe glared silently at Thad and the others. "You know so much about her, maybe you can tell me which one of you fine gentlemen got her in the fix you say she's in."

"We don't know, and she doesn't either," Thad said. "And if she did know, she'd be talking to a lawyer. Can't you see that?"

"All of a sudden you guys seem to have gotten all worked up about my welfare. I haven't heard any of you say anything about Marie's welfare." He started the truck. "All of you take your dirty minds away from here. I've got by this far without following your advice on anything, so I guess I can make it a while longer."

They left and moments later Marie parked at the lumberyard gate in her father's Buick. When Abe walked outside the lumberyard, he leaned down and placed his hand on hers. He could see she had been crying again. He said, "I hope you didn't see those town gossips that just left."

"I saw them," she said. "Are you sure you still want to marry me, Abe?"

"I love you and I guess I always will, come hell or high water, Marie. I don't care about anything but being with you and taking care of you and anything that's yours. I'm not asking you any questions about anything personal, and I don't want any explanations."

With that assurance, the matter was closed, and the next evening, which was on a Friday, they were married with me serving as best man and Becky as bride's maid. It was a small wedding with only Pastor Caruthers, Marie's parents and Becky and I in attendance. Following the ceremony, Abe and Marie left Libbyville with the back seat of his Dodge filled with their personal belongings. Reverend Caruthers told us it was Abe's decision to move from Libbyville, and Marie had agreed. She told Reverend Caruthers she realized that except for the friendship that Abe had enjoyed with me, and the recognition Abe received as a fiddle player, Libbyville held no happy memories for her new husband, and in view of the persistent rumors about her, their marriage had little chance of succeeding there.

Abe had told me virtually the same thing before he climbed into his car, and added, "In spite of all the bad talk, I consider myself the world's luckiest and richest man today." He hesitated. "I believe we can make it, but if we don't, I'm gonna make sure it's not my fault. In any case, if anything ever happens to me, I want you to have my fiddle. You're the only person in Libbyville that's been good to me all my life."

His final remarks only added to my anxieties. It suggested that he too might have reservations about the future of his marriage.

The preacher approached me as they drove away. "Bill, I know you have some concerns about this marriage, so I'll tell you what Abe told me that might give you some comfort. He said all his dreams of ever having a full, happy life were fulfilled when Marie became his wife. He said he considered her to be everything beautiful and sacred in life."

"I'm happy Abe feels that way, but if his marriage fails, it means he'll have a harder fall. I'm wondering if Abe could handle it."

"Abe's an idealist for sure, and he's placing a tremendous responsibility on Marie's shoulders. She is one of God's children, but she's also a human being."

I was sure of one thing. Her marriage to Abe had improved her damaged reputation, and gained her unborn child a good man for its father. All attempts to reassure myself, however, did not eliminate my fear of what Abe might do if Marie betrayed his trust and returned to her former lifestyle.

When at work in my parents' grocery store located on the street behind the Methodist church, I found myself looking frequently at its front entrance, as if some inner force was telling me Abe would reappear there soon.

My job also kept me in touch with most of the families in Libbyville, which allowed me to stay up to date on important events in our little town and hear any news about Abe and Marie. I heard nothing about them for over a year, not even a report on where they were living. I was told by a former classmate, however, that that Marie had made infrequent telephone calls to her mother, but if she had advised her of their whereabouts, the mother did not repeat it to anyone outside her immediate family. When I asked the mother about Abe and Marie one time when she was shopping, she told me that following one of Marie's calls, her daughter's marriage had a better chance at success if no one in Libbyville knew of their whereabouts, because that would prompt calls and other forms of unwanted prying.

My hopes about the marriage of Abe and Marie had begun to grow to the point where I was beginning to feel my fears had been unfounded, when all hopes wee shattered. That's when I glanced at the Methodist's parsonage door and saw a gaunt and unkempt Abe standing there. Reverend Caruthers said later that Abe had an expression of dread and fear on his face like none he had ever seen.

Abe disappeared inside, and as time passed, residents who had noted Abe's presence began driving slowly by. Those who walked to the scene waited anxiously in silence for Abe's reappearance. When he did come out, they said he was so absorbed in thought he did not speak. When Reverend Caruthers did not come outside, their curiosity kept them on the scene. Approximately thirty minutes from the time Abe drove off, a state trooper arrived, then the county sheriff and a deputy. That caused more curious citizens to gather, and I rushed from the store to join them.

We waited anxiously for the officers or Reverend Caruthers to reappear, as more cars and people arrived. The street was now blocked.

When Reverend Caruthers finally came outside followed by the officers, a hush fell over the crowd. For a moment, the only sound heard was the tolling of the church bell announcing the hour, the call of a crow down the street.

Reverend Caruthers's face was grim. "This is indeed a sad day for Libbyville and our church."

A man called out, "What's going on, preacher? Where's Abe? Is Marie with him?"

Reverend Caruthers said, "The sheriff has just told me that Abe is in the hospital in grave condition, and that Marie is dead."

Excited voices rose above all other sounds and the crowd pushed closer. I asked, "Dead? In the hospital? What happened?"

The preacher held up his hand in a plea for silence. "Today's tragic events began with a visit from Abe in my study. He was very frightened. Wanted to know if God would forgive a man for doing something bad if he did it to save somebody else from a life of sin and an eternity in hell. I asked him to be more specific, but his mind had drifted away. I asked him where Marie was and he told me she was waiting for him out at his special place on the edge of town. I asked if she was all right, and he said she was in a safe place now. I asked what he was so disturbed about, and he told me that soon after their baby was born, Marie began running around on him. She had the drug crowd come by and pick her up and give her drugs and God only knows what else. She remained with them all day, and sometimes all night. Most of the time during the next several months, she came home high on drugs, or drunk. One time when he found her at a house in the slums, he pleaded with her to change her ways, and she laughed and told him she'd never stop having fun. He told her, that if she didn't love him enough to change, to change for their baby's sake. She spat at him."

I moaned and shaking my head. My worst fears and Abe's basketball friends proved well founded.

Reverend Caruthers continued. "After much pleading, Abe said he got her to come home to take care of their baby for a short time." He hesitated, obviously dreading what he must say. "Within three weeks, she called her drug using friends and left with them, leaving their child alone in their apartment. She was gone so much after that, Abe said he almost lost his job caring for their baby girl. It was clear that he considered the child to be his too."

A woman asked: "What did he do with the baby?"

"Through a church where they lived, he found an agency that would care for the child that he named Annie Marie Stokes. He began searching for Marie again, and when he found her, he forced her to go home with him, but during the days that followed, he said he saw her riding through town with other men. Said he'd rather be dead than see the angel he loved getting her wings dirtier and dirtier. Said he was already in hell, and she would be too someday, if he couldn't save her from her sinful ways."

"Who shot him?" a man called out. "And who killed Marie?"

"It happened at Abe's favorite place where he taught himself to play his fiddle," the preacher said. "He had told me in my study that he brought Marie to that place in one final attempt to persuade her to change her ways. The idea that he might have already shot her never crossed my mind, but after receiving the sheriff's report, I now know that's what happened. Anyway, after Abe left the sanctuary, I called the sheriff, sensing that something very tragic was about to happen, or already had. I told him about Abe's visit and how he had left very distraught, and where he might find him."

He shook his head. "What a sad day this is."

"What did the sheriff do?" I asked.

"He went to Abe's special place, and when he got there he found Marie lying dead on a bloody blanket an Abe lying next to her crying like a baby with his arm across her. When Abe saw the sheriff's car, he grabbed his pistol and shot himself in the chest."

"Oh my God!" I moaned. "I wish he'd brought Marie to me first."

Reverend Caruthers continued. "The sheriff called an ambulance, and while waiting for it, found a note Abe had left apparently that for those who found their bodies after he took his own life. In it he said he couldn't go on living without the woman he loved, and even if he could, he didn't deserve to live after what he had done."

Reverend Caruthers beckoned to me. "Bill, the officers found another note in Abe's fiddle case that directed the finder to give his fiddle to you, the best friend he ever had in this world. The sheriff said he'd deliver it to you when his investigation is completed."

The crowd slowly dispersed, talking in hushed tones about what had happened. Some of the men came by our store to express their opinions on what Abe had done. They all agreed that he had done a bad thing, but they understood why he had done it, and if their wives had done what Marie had done, they were not sure they wouldn't have reacted the same way.

I attempted to see Abe in the hospital in the county seat, but because he was still near death, no visitors were allowed. After being told by a hospital spokesman that Abe would recover, I returned later, but was told Abe's state of mind was such that he should not yet talk to anyone not connected to the criminal investigation. Several days later, I was allowed to visit Abe, but I was not prepared for the shock of seeing my boyhood friend in such a sad state. He broke down and cried upon seeing me, but upon regaining his composure he told me to pull up a chair and spend some time with him.

He apologized for disappointing me so, telling me he wished he had died for taking the life of the only woman he would ever love and prayed that God would provide a long and happy life for his baby. He told me he would plead guilty when he went to court and asked the judge to sentence him to death.

He asked me to apologize to our basketball team for what he had done, and do the same when I saw Reverend Caruthers and the owner of the lumber company. With a sad face, he said, "Tell our preacher to pray for my soul which I know is lost forever." He told me he had been praying, but he had been so bad he doubted God was listening. He stated the doubted God would ever visit him again, anywhere or any time. He shook my hand.

Abe be survived his wounds, and six weeks later a deputy sheriff escorted him to the courthouse in handcuffs. Refusing a court appointed attorney, he plead guilty to the murder charge and asked to sentence him to death. Instead, the judge sentenced him to forty years after hearing pleas for mercy from many responsible people from Libbyville, including me. Abe thanked all those who said kind words about him and asked all those who did to pray that his baby would have a full and happy life and love him in spite of what he had done.

I departed for college shortly thereafter, and after graduation moved to another city to work for a national grocery chain. I therefore heard no more about Abe from the people in Libbyville. Upon visiting my parents during my first semester break, I did learn that Abe's family and all their relatives had either died or moved away. During the following years, I was unable to determine if Abe died in prison or was paroled, and if he was, where he lived.

After what seemed like days instead of hours at the mountain landing, we boarded the cable car for the return trip to the Gatlinburg landing. The trip was painfully slow. Upon arriving there, I rushed to the waiting area to look for Abe, but did not find him. With the other car now back on the mountain, I could not ask its operator if Abe got my message.

Refusing to believe Abe would not want to meet with me, I asked the ticket agent if she had talked to a tall, stooped man with white hair who had come down from the mountain in the other car.

The lady smiled. "He got your message and said to tell you he had another appointment he could not miss. Said to ask you to meet him at our concert hall tonight after eight. He'll reserve you a seat on the front row."

Pleased that I would see my old friend after all, many questions came to mind. When was he released from prison? Is he physically and mentally well? What is he doing here? Did his ex-convict status compel him to take a menial maintenance job at the park? Maybe he is a janitor. I wished I had his fiddle with me.

Looking about for someone who might be working for the park, I approached a young man with a logo on is shirt and asked him, "Did you see a tall, white-headed, older man get out of the car that just left?"

The young man looked at me. "What was he wearing?"

"A white shirt is all I could see. He has white hair. Was bare headed. He has a long, sad face and is stooped shoulders."

He smiled. "You must be talking about the Fiddling' Man."

My adrenaline surged as memories of Libbyville swept over me. "He does play a fiddle.

"That's what we call him at the park. We see him around pretty often. He plays a fiddle here, and over at Dollywood. Man, can that man play a fiddle! And the lady that plays the guitar with him is a real looker. Yeah, I saw him. He waited around a while before that lady picked him up."

The young man pointed. "See that poster on the light pole? That'll tell you where you can hear him and the lady play."

On the poster dated July 4, 2016, I found a picture of Abe's sad face, wrinkled with age, and one of a very pretty lady with black hair, brown eyes and fair complexion. Abe was holding a fiddle and a bow in one hand, and the lady held a guitar. She was smiling.

Words across the bottom of the poster read: Abe and Annie Marie Stokes are appearing again on the stages of Gatlinburg and Dollywood to repeat their stunning performance of the beloved American folk songs and tunes of the South and the Appalachian area. Dates and times were listed.

My pulse was beating faster now. The name Annie Marie rang a bell in my memory bank. Of course! It was Marie Tidwell's child, the baby that Abe had taken as his own.

Studying the picture more closely, I found how much the pretty lady favored her mother. So much, that her presence must make Abe feel like he is still with the woman he aid he would love forever.

God had visited Abe after all.

I was anxious to find out the circumstances of their meeting following his release, and if she was told how mother died. Did she love him half as much as Abe loved Marie? There were so many questions he had to ask his old friend.

I remembered Marie's mother telling me Abe had placed their baby with an agency in the Texas hill country when he started having so much trouble with her mother. Had she remained at the agency until grown, or was she adopted? Was she married? Did she have a family? How long after his release did Abe wait before reuniting with her? Married or single, the smile on her face in the picture told me Abe finally could claim that he now had a family that loved him.

I would get to the concert hall early and claim my reserved seat, and after the concert, I would meet with my old friend for a long talk about his and his daughter's life following his release, and all the other things that had enriched his life since he had returned to the free world.

I would give him his old fiddle that my dear, departed wife Becky had kept dry and polished in her cedar chest in our home. It would be a very good day.

Uncle Willy's Garage Sale

Retired high school agriculture teacher Willy Dowd looked at the Garage Sale sign through the glass storm door of his living room.

"Ridiculous," he muttered. "It might as well read funeral arrangements pending. Why did I allow my daughter to advertise my approaching demise?"

He was glad the sale would not start until one o'clock the next day after his daughter Amelia arrived and set up things for the ordeal. He dreaded the invasion of his home by strangers who would rush in like charging beasts to jerk, turn and toss, and otherwise insult those items he and his Nellie had acquired during forty years of marriage. Like a thief in the night, old age and rheumatism had delivered him to that time in his life when all men must release material things and hold on to hope.

Where did all the time go? He wished he still had his Nellie. A man's life is not complete without a good wife to support him.

A blue Ford slowed down near the sign, stopped and backed up, then pulled into the driveway. His first impulse was to close the main door and refuse to open it when the intruder knocked. Didn't the driver read the sign?

He was pulling the metal door forward when an attractive lady climbed out of the car. Rather short and plump with wavy grey hair down to her collar, she reminded him of his Nellie. He re-opened the door and looked past the tall tarp covered object near the steps to get a clearer view of the lady. It had been a lonesome life since his Nellie died.

The pretty lady walked briskly across the porch and knocked gently on the glass door. He opened it.

"Good morning, pretty lady. May I help you?"

She smiled, showing even white teeth. There wasn't a wrinkle in her face. "I'm here about your garage sale."

"But it doesn't begin until noon tomorrow."

She smiled again. "I read the sign, but I have to be in Austin by two o'clock to close on my home and furniture I'm selling there, and since I won't be back for several days, I was hoping you might allow me to look at what you're selling that I could use in the house I'll be buying where I'll be near my daughter."

"I'd be happy to, but the house is a mess. Come in."

She stopped inside and offered her hand. "I'm Beatrice. Bea for short."

He took her soft hand and felt an unaccustomed rush. "Willy Dowd. Everybody calls me Uncle Willy."

"That's nice, but since you're not old enough to be my uncle, I'll call you Willie. Okay?" She turned to admire his glistening wood floor and living room furnishings. "It's beautiful."

She stepped over to the Windberg painting of a broken wooden gate leading to an old, leaning barn with a roof of rotten, wood shingles. "I love Windbergs."

She approached a table on which was located a glass case containing a violin and a bow. A picture of a smiling Nellie was beside it. "Your wife?"

"Yes. Her name was Winell, but I called her Nellie."

"I'd like to meet her if she's here."

"She was killed eight years ago when a drunk drier crossed over the center stripe and hit her head on. God allowed him to live and Nellie to die. She was horribly mutilated and in intense pain for three days."

"How terrible. She played that violin?"

"Up until she died I played the fiddle, but when she was killed, I put it in that case and never played it again."

She held his gaze a moment, obviously feeling his pain. "Are there any more tributes to her that I should watch out for so I won't disgrace them by bumping into them?"

He nodded toward the front door. "I threw a tarp over a concrete cross after God allowed the crazy driver to live and my Nellie to die. She was horribly mangled, and suffered severe pain for several days."

"I wondered what that was. Are you still mad at God?"

"Mad and skeptical. If He has the power to save people, why didn't He save my Christian wife instead of the wrong-doer?"

"I wouldn't dare speak for God. And I won't deny that there are some things I don't understand either. That's why I try to concentrate instead on the beautiful things around me."

He admired her perfect posture and her straightforwardness. "I admire you for that. If you'll have a cup of coffee with me later, maybe some of your positive way of thinking will wear off on me."

"I'd love that." Her smile was very uplifting. It reminded him of how he felt in the presence of his Nellie.

He walked to the hall door. "Follow me and I'll show you some things. What will you need?"

"A bedroom suite, and since I let my everyday china and silverware go with my Austin house, I'll also need some replacements."

He pointed. "Kitchen is last room down the hall."

He saw her glance at another Windberg near the entrance to the kitchen. Through a connecting door to the dining room she could see some of his best silverware his daughter had already removed from the cabinet.

"You're selling your best silverware?"

"Letting it go will be much easier than loosing other things I've lost. A grumpy old man alone doesn't need fine silver."

"But you may marry again. All wives love fine silverware." She glanced at him as if she might have something else in mind beside the silverware. "Why don't we look at a bedroom suite first? That'll give you more time to think about it."

He led her up the hall to the first bedroom. "We bought this mahogany suite when I got my first teaching job. The others are a bit newer, but not as grand. You might prefer this one. Beauty for the beautiful."

She dazzled him again with her smile. "Thank you." She gently moved her hand over the chenille bedspread on her way to the dresser. "It's something to be proud of. You won't need it in the home you're moving to?"

"I'll have no use for it. I'm moving to a dying home."

She gave him a shocked look. "You don't look like a sick man to me."

"Some people call them retirement or assisted living homes"

She breathed a sigh of relief. "You scared me. Some of my friends live in them. They're nice. Why do you call them dying homes?'

"Because that's where a man gives up his independence, and the last place where he lives before he dies."

"The same thing could be said of this home, if it's where you choose to live the rest of your life. My goodness!"

"Funny how I never looked at it that way."

"Always look on the bright side of things, Willy. If you don't see it some days, be patient. Look harder. Every day is a gift from God."

"You really think so?"

"I prefer to believe so. When you're troubled by negative thoughts, ask yourself, 'Could humans have made all the wonderful things we see around us every day? Could man have made something as perfect as the human body, or that of animals and bugs?'"

"And drunk drivers?"

"He gave us brains to allow us to prevent bad things. That's one of those man things that happen when man doesn't use what God gave him." She studied him a moment. "Have you ever thought about how much happier you could be if you'd stop trying to reinvent the wheel and living in the past? Forgive yourself and move on." She placed her hand on his arm. "Forgive me for giving you a lecture. I'm sorry."

"I never get upset over a good woman giving me advice."

"You know what they say. Life is what you make it. You still have lots of good years left. I'll bet you're not a day over fifty-five."

"Sixty-eight. Too old and ugly to think I might one day have a smart, pretty woman like you as a partner."

"Don't be so hard on yourself." She looked at his wife's picture on the chest of drawers. "I feel like an intruder looking at this bedroom suite. Do you have another?"

"Next room. But it's maple."

"I'll take it. Can we go on into the kitchen now?" She glanced at her watch. "Have to be at the closing at two."

"Follow me." He walked ahead of her down to the kitchen. He pulled back two chairs from the table laden with two cereal bowls, a plate and some silverware he had used for breakfast. He pushed them back. "Sorry. Have a seat."

She sat down and placing her purse at her feet. It was something he had often seen his Nellie do. The occasion was made more poignant by Bea choosing the chair nearest his. When he saw her look at Nellie's favorite iron skillet he used to fry his eggs, he moved it to the counter. "I'll make us some coffee so you won't bet sleepy driving to Austin."

She jumped up. "You will not. That's a woman's job. Just show me where everything is."

The longer he was with her, the more he admired her. How many women in the modern world still considered serving men to be a woman's responsibility?

He must stop thinking like a sentimental old fool and move on. That's what she said he should do. Stop dwelling on events of the past.

He watched her in silence as she went about making the coffee and moving the dirty dishes to the sink. He wanted to say something clever, but could not think of anything but, "My everyday stuff is in those drawers along the kitchen counter." What a boring thing to say at such a critical time.

She found two cups and the creamer, poured the coffee and sat down opposite him. "Is it too weak or too strong?"

"It's just right. Thank you."

They sipped and looked nervously about as the Grandmother clock in the dining room ticked softly.

He said, "Sorry I don't have some cookies."

"Just coffe is enough. I don't need the extra calories."

"You have a great figure." It had slipped out. "Excuse me. I didn't mean to sound fresh."

She smiled. "Thank you."

"I'd like to see you again." The words had slipped out again, as if a power from with had taken over to express his inner yearnings.

"Thank you for the flattery." She smiled. It was not the response he had hoped to hear.

She looked at the neatly stacked dishes and cooking utensils through the glass cabinet doors. She pointed. "Did you arrange all those things?"

"No. There are some things men don't do well. The world would fall apart and all the lights would go out without good women to make the world complete."

"You're an idealist from the old school in some ways, I've noticed."

"And proud of it. Is that bad?"

"Not necessarily, but it clashes with what you did to that cross out front. Old school conservatives are usually devoted Christians. They claim to be, at least."

"One never knows what kind of pie is on his table until he opens the crust. Somebody should invent an honesty pen that laws would require all men to wear in public places. When they lie, it would make a loud, screeching noise."

She laughed. "You're funny."

"Old enough to be on Medicare and still looking for answers. Too bad doctors don't have a prescription for correct answers to all questions."

"You're one of those skeptics who want to solve all the mysteries of life and take away all the excitement of living. Relax and enjoy. Stop trying to find answers to every question." She turned. "May I look at your kitchen ware now so I can get on my way and you can do what you need to do to get ready for your big day tomorrow?"

"Help yourself. You'll find everything in those cabinets and drawers that's not setting out already."

She stopped to admire the heavy iron skillet near the stove. "My mother and grandmother had one of these," she said as she moved her fingers along the rim.

"It's yours. And anything else you like."

"Thank you." She selected two pans, some knives, spoons and forks, two boilers, four glasses and cups, and a large white pitcher.

After placing her selections in a neat arrangement on the counter, she picked up her purse. "I must be going now. Thank you for the coffee and for allowing me to go through your belongings. You are very kind."

"May I call you sometimes?"

Her eyes met his. "I would like that. I'll give you my daughter's number." She wrote the number on a napkin and placed it on the table.

He accompanied her to her car and opened the door, telling her, "I have very much enjoyed visiting with you, Bea. Made me realize just how empty my life has been. And since I won't know when you'll be back, will you please call me and let me know? I'm in the directory."

"Will you still be in this house?" He thought he detected a note of hope in what she said.

He glanced at the garage sale sign. "If you'll promise to call me the first day you're back, I'll pull up that sign."

She smiled and got in the car. "You funny man. It's a deal."

He patted her hand on the steering wheel. "Bye, pretty woman. Have a safe trip."

She backed into the street, waved and drove away. When her car disappeared around the next corner, he pulled up the sign and tossed it behind the hedges near the front porch. He then very carefully pulled the faded blue tarp from the white concrete cross. He folded it and tossed it on a shelf in the garage. After he drank another cup of coffee he would pull up the grass and weeds that had grown tall around the base of the cross while under the tarp.